HEART AND SOUL OF THE WOLF

GUARDIAN OF THE WINTER STONE

ARIANA JADE

ARIZONA TAPE

Copyright © 2024 by Ariana Jade & Arizona Tape

All rights reserved. No part of this publication or cover may be reproduced, distributed, or transmitted in any form or by any means, including photocopying, recording, or other electronic or mechanical methods, without the prior written permission of the publisher, except in the case of brief quotations embodied in critical reviews and certain other noncommercial uses permitted by copyright law.

The scanning, uploading, and distribution of this book without permission is a theft of the author's copyrighted work and intellectual property.

If you would like permission to use material from the book, then please write to Arizona Tape at arizonatape@arizonatape.com

Heart And Soul Of The Wolf is a work of fiction. Names, characters, businesses, places, events, locales, and incidents are either the products of the author's imagination or used in a fictitious manner. Any resemblance to actual persons, living or dead, businesses, companies, locales, or actual events is purely coincidental.

Individuals depicted in the images and cover are models and used solely for illustrative purposes.

Cover By Vampari Designs

Visit the author's website here: https://arizonatape.com

If you've found any errors, you can report them here. Please note that my books are written in British English.

You can keep up to date with news about releases and deals by subscribing to Arizona Tape's newsletter or joining her reader group, Rainbow Central.

BLURB

Mayu is equal parts lucky and unlucky.

As one of the few people with a wolf soul, she was chosen to go on a sacred quest to retrieve the Winter Stone. It's a long dangerous journey but she doesn't have to undertake it alone. Her best friend since childhood, Konomi, is accompanying her.

As much as Mayu loves having someone by her side, she's also desperately in love with Konomi and to make matters worse, she's her sister-in-law.

Will this journey be one of love or heartbreak?

Heart And Soul Of The Wolf is a f/f romance with lots of gay panic, a little bit of steam, and no cheating.

It serves as a prequel to the Guardian Of The Winter Stone series.

ONE

I swung my bow over my shoulder, making sure it was securely in place before I even attempted to climb up the steep hill. My long hair tangled in front of my face and I wished I'd tied it up before attempting this. The cave wasn't the easiest to reach but the risk was worth it. It looked promising and we needed a place to sleep for the night, one that wasn't under the stars.

"And?" a light voice shouted from behind me.

"I think it looks good," I called back. I put my bow and quiver down against a rock and reached down, holding out my hand to the most beautiful woman I'd ever met, trying to ignore how stunning she looked in the falling light of the winter sun.

Konomi smiled at me in a way that creased her eyes slightly. "Thank you, Mayu. You're the best sister-in-law."

The words squeezed my heart like a tight fist and I quickly let go of her hand, feeling guilty for even looking at her like that. The wolf soul in me reacted differently, wanting the closeness, but I couldn't listen to that part of me. Luckily, the cave was dark so she wouldn't be able to see the redness rising to my cheeks.

She pointed down at our packs leaning against a tree. "We can bring those up in a moment, right?"

"Yes, let's look around the cave first," I said. It wouldn't be the first time on our journey that we'd entered a cave that was unsuitable, or worse, occupied.

With Konomi by my side, I ventured further into the hollow structure. There was a limited amount of space where we could stand in before the walls came together to form the ceiling. But it was dry, empty, and most of all, shelter from the elements. While the weather was beautiful now, night came quickly this time of year.

"I think we can stay the night here," I said.

"I agree. I hope there's a bath," Konomi said, as always quick with a joke.

I didn't know what I would do without her lightness. Her company and persisting brightness were one of the few things that was making this long impossible journey bearable. If she hadn't been here, I was sure I would've given up a long time ago. If only I could tell her just how much she meant to me.

I shook the traitorous thoughts away and clambered down to gather the rest of our belongings. We travelled light by necessity, but after a full day of walking, those packs were the heaviest thing in the world. While I brought everything up to the cave, Konomi started a fire. She was always much better at that, at anything that required patience.

It didn't take long for the fire to light up the cave and chase away the chill. I sank down on a cleared bit of ground, relieved to be off my feet. Travelling through dense forest was my least favourite and the Alladwin forest was certainly that. Dense.

Konomi settled next to me and handed me a raw fish skewered on a stick. "Here."

A smile made its way to my tired lips as I held it over the flames. "Thank you. You take good care of me."

"That's my job, isn't it?" She dipped her head lightly, her tone teasing. "Guardian."

"Don't call me that."

"Why? That's what you are. Honoured Guardian of the Winter Stone."

I sarcastically gestured to the empty space in front of me. "Do you *see* the Winter Stone? No. So until we've actually found it, don't call me the Guardian. I'm a Guardian of nothing."

Konomi's smile slipped away and I instantly felt bad for snapping at her. It wasn't her fault that we were alone together on an impossible quest or that this cave was so small, our knees were touching.

I shot her an apologetic grimace. "Sorry, that was uncalled for. Especially because you didn't have to come on this quest with me. I'm just tired and tense."

"I know. I forgive you." Her genuine smile showed that she meant it too.

We rested in silence with nothing but the crackling of the fire as the darkness swallowed everything outside the cave. Once the skin of my fish was blistered and blackened, I shot a prayer to the Great Wolf before I started eating. It wasn't anywhere close to a full meal but we hadn't had that privilege for a long time.

After a while, Konomi spoke, her voice thin and devoid of all earlier lightness. "How many days more are we going to be stuck in this forest?"

I tossed my empty stick into the fire, watching it catch fire. "I don't know."

"Maybe we should go back."

"To that village with the leery old men? I don't think that would be a good idea." I reached into my pack for the weathered map of the area, although as we quickly discovered, it was rather inaccurate. "If we keep travelling east with the river, we should reach the Red Boar Inn eventually."

Konomi let out a pensive hum. "And what if we're following the wrong river?"

"We're not," I assured her, somehow managing to sound confident.

"But what if we are?"

"I promise you, we're not."

"All right. I trust you." She pulled her knees up to her chin, her gaze locked onto the crackling fire.

A silence fell over us, the kind that only existed in the quiet of winter. Somewhere, a lone owl hooted into the night.

Konomi's sigh sounded like it came from deep within. "Mayu?"

The way she said my name tightened my chest but I didn't let it show. "Yes?"

"This Winter Stone better be worth it."

The faintest of smiles curled my lips up and I could only nod in agreement because it was better if my true feelings on the matter never saw the light of day.

TWO

The freezing cold made my fingers tremble more than normal and the arrow flying from my bow veered too far to the right. It startled the rabbit and the skittish animal darted away, only leaving little footprints in the snow as proof that I hadn't imagined its presence.

So close.

I retrieved the missed arrow, only to find the tip broken off. It seemed like it was just one of those days where everything went wrong. My stomach tightened painfully, as if I needed another reminder why I couldn't keep missing my shots.

Determined, I followed the trail of little bunny prints. One of the benefits of snow. I tracked it through the forest, making notches in the trees so I wouldn't get lost. It didn't take long before I spotted the quick-footed animal again, sitting near a bush where it was nibbling on some of the lowest branches.

I reached for another arrow and slowly raised my bow. With practised ease, I slipped the arrow in its place and took aim. There was almost no breeze and I had a clear shot. Instead of letting go, I breathed hot air on my fingers until they felt less stiff.

With a sharp breath in, I let go of the arrow. There wasn't enough time for a prayer but I didn't need it. I could feel it the moment the arrow left, I could tell from the sound of my bow string.

The arrow sank into the rabbit's eye and killed the small animal in one clean shot. This time, I did whisper a prayer to the Great Wolf to thank him for blessing me. This rabbit would be a very welcome dinner.

As much as I wanted to keep hunting, mostly out of pride instead of hunger, I knew venturing too far away from Konomi and our camp was not a good idea. If we got separated from each other, that would be a real reason to panic.

I retraced my steps by following the notches in the trees, relieved when I spotted the fire in the cave. I had my father to thank for teaching me how to hunt and move through a forest even though I was a girl. Not wanting to get caught up in thoughts of my family, I pushed the fond memories away before they could turn bitter. As much as I was sure that my parents and younger brother would love to know I was missing them, out here, getting distracted could be the death of me.

Konomi looked up from her spot in the cave, a smile rising to her red lips. She looked so beautiful even in the poor state we were in. There was just a twinkle in her eyes, a lift to her lips that shone through regardless of the grime, dirt, and hollowness of her face.

She lowered the coat she was mending, careful not to lose the needle. "Welcome home."

She had no idea how much I wanted her to say that for real but there was no way we would ever share a home. Not a real one anyway.

"The rabbits were elusive but not elusive enough," I said, keeping a safe distance as I held up my prey. "I also found some mushrooms so we won't starve tonight." I handed her the rabbit and the satchel with my finds.

"We won't starve but we might die," Konomi said, holding up one of the mushrooms with a tethered cap. "These are poisonous."

"Are they?" I frowned. "I thought they were common brown mushrooms."

"See the gills?" She showed me the underside. "Common brown mushrooms don't have these white spores on them."

With a sigh, I sank down by the fire. "What would I do without you?"

Konomi gave me a good-natured smile. "Knowing you, you wouldn't have even made it to the Flower Village. This is probably why the Elders allow family to join in on the sacred quest."

Family. I loved the word as much as I hated it. Even though we were in the middle of nowhere, she would always be my sister-in-law. Worse. My older brother's widow. The guilt encompassed me and I prayed that my brother couldn't watch us from beyond the grave. If he knew how I was looking at his wife…

"So what are our plans?" Konomi asked, snapping me from my thoughts.

"I think we should stay here one more night and then continue on. I'm sick of this forest. I want a real bed, a roof over our head, a hot meal that's actually filling. And a bath." I sighed just thinking of the hot water. I couldn't remember the last time I had a relaxing soak but it must have been over two months ago, from before we left home for this foolish quest to find the Winter Stone.

Konomi finished mending the jacket and put it aside. "I feel quite rested. I'll see if I can catch some fish."

I nodded. "That's a good idea. I'll keep the fire going so you can warm up when you're back. I need to make some more arrows, I broke two of them earlier today."

A grave look appeared on Konomi's beautiful face. "We're not in the best shape, are we?"

"No, but I would say we've done remarkably well considering we're only nineteen and twenty-two. We're on the biggest journey of our life without much experience or help. Before all this, I thought the forest near our village was as far as the wide world went and you were teaching children how to count. Not exactly seasoned travellers, are we?"

Konomi smiled. "You're right. And look at us now. I bet the village will be astounded when they hear our stories."

"If we ever make it back," I said darkly. When the village briefed me, it wasn't lost on me that we weren't allowed to return empty handed.

"*When* we make it back. When we return with the Winter Stone, we'll surely be given a hero's welcome. Better, a Guardian's welcome. I can't wait to see everyone again, especially your parents. They were always so kind to me, even after..." Konomi didn't manage to finish her sentence, but she didn't have to.

I knew what she meant, I was there to witness it all. My parents falling to pieces, Konomi losing her husband, my younger brother's first experience with death. My own grief. And how I was tainting those memories by harbouring misguided feelings for his widow. Even if nothing would ever happen, could happen, I definitely didn't deserve a hero's welcome.

The weight in my stomach grew even heavier as Konomi got up from the fire and took my hand in hers. It was warm from the fire and fitted mine perfectly.

"I'm so glad I have you," she said, sounding so painfully genuine, it was heartbreaking.

"And I you," I replied earnestly. No matter how inappropriate my feelings were, I would not have made it this far without her. Her warmth, her companionship, her ability to identify poisonous mushrooms, they were all invaluable to me. Without her, I would've long lost the strength and motivation to keep going on this seemingly endless journey.

She let go of my hand and flashed me her toothy grin. "Now let's hope the fish are biting."

"Good luck. I'll be here when you get back." Because no matter my feelings, we were in this together. This quest for the sacred Winter Stone that somehow had fallen on my shoulders. All because I had the soul of a wolf.

THREE

The next day, we resumed our journey at daybreak. According to the map and the directions from the locals, we just needed to follow the river to reach the other end of the forest. I sincerely hoped that was true because this dense forest was disorienting and I had enough of it.

For most of the morning, we walked alongside the river in the hope it would bring us to the elusive inn. I loved being near the water. There was something about the way that it reflected the sunlight and the world, ever so slightly distorted but real, that made it so mysterious. When I looked down at it, at my own face, my own eyes, I always felt like the water made it seem like there was slumbering something underneath. As if I stared long enough, the wolf soul within me would look back. As a child, I'd sat by the river's edge many times to test out that theory but nothing ever happened.

Konomi hummed a soft tune as she followed a trail, somehow making it look like she was dancing instead of struggling. It would never cease to amaze me how she could remain so upbeat when we were hungry, tired, and cold.

We had lunch on a flat rock and Konomi took advantage of the sun to try and spear some fish. She didn't succeed but she seemed to have fun. I wasn't so foolish as to believe that her having fun was more important than us having food but it was definitely a lovely thing to see. It made me wonder what the other people I cared for were doing at this exact moment. Were my parents coping? Was my little brother growing up well?

It was impossible to know but I held them close in my heart. I was on this mission for them, for our village. My family's safety was the most important thing to me.

My gaze went to Konomi who looked so breathtakingly beautiful, it ached.

My family and *her*. Even if she could never know.

It was late afternoon when I noticed the thin trail of smoke rising in the distance.

"Fire!" Konomi's shout made birds flutter up from their nests. "That has to be the inn!"

"It might not be," I said, not quite as ready to celebrate. One of us had to be the realist, we couldn't both be dreamers.

Still, there was just a little bit of extra bounce in my step as we hiked further down. We took less breaks than we usually would, fuelled by hope and the promise of a good meal, a bath, a night under a roof.

It was evening by the time we reached the valley and darkness was descending over us. It would have been wise to make camp for the night but neither of us suggested it. Instead, we continued stubbornly towards the beacon of smoke. As it got darker, Konomi fashioned a torch from a tree branch, some resin, and a bit of cloth. It was foolish to walk in bad visibility, I could hear my father's warnings in my ear, but I didn't heed any of them. I just followed Konomi and the torch she was carrying like I would die if I had to spend one more night under the stars.

She came to an abrupt halt and I almost knocked into her.

"By the Great Wolf, it *is* an inn. We found it!" Her voice rose slightly. "Mayu! You genius!"

I managed a tired but satisfied smile. "Told you it was the right river."

The inn was nestled in a clearing, protected by the river on one side and a steep mountain on the other that reminded me a little of the sacred mountain at home. The location made the inn impossible to miss and that in itself was a relief that we hadn't walked past it without knowing. It looked old but robust, like it had weathered centuries and was ready for plenty more to come. The windows were lit up from the fire inside and a small trail led right down to the front door. A wooden board hung next to it, one with a red boar painted on it.

An instant sense of relief filled me when we entered. I could smell food and hear the gentle crackle of a hearth. Simple pleasures of life but right now, a genuine life line. It was so warm inside compared to the bitter cold, it was making my fingers and ears tingle. While we always slept by a campfire, nothing beat the real all encompassing warmth of being inside a house. I could tell from the expression on Konomi's face that she felt exactly the same.

A man with a long grey beard was sitting at one

of the tables, smoke from his pipe surrounding his face. He looked up when we entered and shot us a smile. "Oh? Travellers?"

Konomi stepped forward, bowing slightly. "Good evening. I hope we're not intruding. We were hoping to stay here for the night, if that's possible."

She spoke the old language fluently, which was to be expected from a priest's daughter and someone as intelligent as her. It sounded lovely coming from her. Not quite as melodic as our own language but that was part of the appeal.

The greying man chuckled. "You best believe it's possible. Ever since my great-great grandfather opened the Red Boar Inn, we haven't turned away a single traveller and I'm not about to start now." He shouted towards an open door. "Rudeus, we have guests!"

Stumbling announced someone else's arrival and another man appeared with a stumpy nose and not a single strand of hair on his head. His smile was wide and welcoming, which reminded me of my grandfather. "Guests! Wonderful! How long are you two staying?"

Konomi glanced at me before she replied. "It depends whether you'll accept chores and help as payment for a bed and a meal. We can cook, clean, hunt, gather, whatever you need."

The bald man, Rudeus, chuckled. "When you're our age, you can always use help. Especially because Mason's back is not what it used to be. You two look tired. Come, sit down. If you're after a meal, we have rabbit stew that needs eating."

I could feel the relief rush through me. It was such a weight off my shoulders to be here, to know that the worst part of the journey was behind us because the Alladwin Forest was certainly one of the more traitorous places I'd ever been in.

We didn't take our shoes off as we entered the main room, they didn't do that in this region of the world. We settled at the long table where Mason was smoking his pipe.

It didn't take long for Rudeus to arrive with two plates that smelled mouth-wateringly amazing. He set them down in front of us without demanding payment up front.

Before we had any chance to dig in, Mason put his pipe down. "Say, by any chance, are you two from near the sacred Yirobi Mountain?"

The mention of our home made me freeze. Before I could think of how to answer, Rudeus swatted the back of Mason's head affectionately. "Mase. You can see how tired these poor girls are. Save your questions for the morning. Don't mind him. Eat up."

And just like that, my appetite was gone.

FOUR

I pushed a chair under the door handle, securing it in place just in case. The last thing I needed was an intruder to come into our room while we slept.

"Don't you think that's unnecessary?" Konomi asked from her bed.

"I don't trust these men," I replied, searching the room for anything else I could use. The dresser looked like it was made of solid wood and one push against it proved it was too heavy to move. I just had to hope that the chair would be sufficient. Maybe I was overreacting. I was so tired, it was hard to think straight.

Konomi came over to me, her hand landing on my arm. "I won't let anything happen to you, Mayu. You know I sleep with a dagger."

I managed a faint smile. "I'm aware. It's just... Don't you think it's weird that they guessed exactly where we're from?"

"Not exactly. They didn't mention our village by name. Just the mountain."

"Still, it's a very very good guess."

"Maybe a lucky guess." Mayu urged me to turn around, her eyes seeking out mine. "I'm sure they'll have a perfectly good explanation in the morning. Let's just get a good night's sleep so if something does happen, we're well rested."

"You're so much kinder than I am. I hope you're right," I conceded.

"I know I'm right," Konomi said, her voice soft and confident at the same time. She gently pulled me away from the door and pushed me towards the bed on the right. "Go on, undress so you can go to sleep."

After travelling together for three months, we had few secrets left between us. Still, I stripped quickly, glad that there was only a single candle in the room. It wasn't my body that I was worried about, it was hers and making her uncomfortable by accidentally staring longer than a friend should.

I slipped into the bed and squeezed my eyes shut while Konomi blew out the candle. I only dared open them when I heard the rustle of fabric and the slight creak of the wooden frame that meant she had gone to bed too.

She let out a contented sigh, so soft it gave me goosebumps. I was such a bad friend.

I turned on my side, facing away from her in the hope that I would fall asleep quickly. I was so tired, it shouldn't be too hard.

"It's nice to be in a bed with a mattress," Konomi said, her voice drifting over to me. She sounded different when she was tired, slightly hoarse.

I loved listening to her like that.

She continued without needing an answer. "I think this rabbit stew might've been my favourite since we've gone on this journey. No offence."

Even without looking at her, I knew she was grinning.

I chuckled lightly. "I'll remember that next time I almost break my neck chasing after one."

"I'd rather you didn't break your neck," she said. Then she added something so softly, I wasn't sure it was intended for my ears. "I wouldn't know what to do without you."

I pretended I hadn't heard that. "How long do you think we should stay here?"

Konomi sighed. "I don't know. It depends on how long they'll let us stay without payment. I can help out in the kitchen and if you get lucky hunting, I'm sure we won't be too much of a burden. It'll be good for us to recharge."

"Unless they kill us tomorrow."

A nervous giggle came from the other bed. "Mayu!"

"What? It's possible."

"If that's what they wanted, they could've done that tonight. You shouldn't see the worst in people." A rustling sound came from Konomi's side of the room. "Do you remember when we met?"

An image of a much younger Konomi flickered through my mind. In my memory, she was shorter and her hair was longer, but her smile was still exactly the same. I'd fallen at first sight.

"What about that first meeting?" I asked, pushing the nostalgic thoughts away.

"You were making blankets for the flowers in your garden so they would survive winter. That kindness was one of the things that drew me to you."

"You mean that foolishness. Flowers don't survive winter for a reason."

Konomi's laugh filled the room. "Foolish or not, it was kind. When I saw that, I knew I wanted us to be friends."

Friends.

I tightened my hands. "Why are you bringing this up now?"

"To remind you that you're a kind person too. Don't change now." Her sheets rustled again. "Mayu? Can you turn around?"

Despite myself and my resolve, I shifted on my other side so I could look at her. Silver moon light streamed in through a narrow window, providing just enough brightness so I could see her face. She was so beautiful, it ached. She reached her hand out to me and I took it, bridging the gap between our beds.

Konomi's eyes shimmered in the moonlight. "I'm so glad we became friends."

"Me too," I whispered.

She squeezed my hand. "I'm so grateful we're family because if we weren't, I couldn't have come on this journey with you."

The image of my older brother's face drove away the warm feeling in my chest. If only he knew…

I swallowed the lump in my throat away while my heart pounded uncontrollably in my chest. "I'm grateful that you're here too. We should go to sleep. You must be tired."

Konomi hummed as she closed her eyes. "I am. Goodnight, Mayu. Sleep well."

She was still holding my hand.

"Sleep well," I whispered, wishing I had the strength and resolve to let go, but I couldn't. Instead, I fell asleep with our hands clasped together, floating in the small gap between us that might as well have been a chasm.

Some things just weren't meant to be.

FIVE

When morning came, the chair was undisturbed. Konomi was gracious enough not to say *I told you so* but her smile was just a little extra wide. Or maybe that was just the effect of having a good night's sleep in a real bed.

The smell of fresh bread lured us downstairs where Rudeus and Mason greeted us in the main room. To my relief, there were other guests at the tables, including some women and even a small child. Maybe my worry last night had been for nothing but I maintained that it was better to be safe than sorry. Especially given the circumstances.

Konomi greeted the owners of the inn with a polite nod before settling at the end of one of the long tables. I took the seat opposite from her and it didn't take long for Rudeus to appear with two plates laden with dried sausages, cheese, and bread generously topped with rich butter. A heavy start to the day but that seemed to be how they enjoyed their breakfasts in this part of the world. It came accompanied by a tankard of beer, another strange custom from around here.

I pressed my hands together to thank the Great Wolf for our meal and dug in without wasting any time. The bread was freshly baked with a golden brown crust and the butter was heavily salted which made it delicious. The spices in the sausage were unfamiliar, more earthy than back home, but it worked wonderfully with the aged cheese.

"I'm going to miss bread when we're back," Konomi said as she devoured her slice in a very unlady-like fashion.

"We have bread at home. Also, you have some butter on your nose." I touched my own unnecessarily. She knew where her nose was.

Konomi wiped the splotch away. "It doesn't taste the same at home. Maybe because I've never been this hungry in my life."

I tore my slice of bread in half and put the biggest part on the rim of her plate. "Have some of mine, then. If you enjoy it that much."

A smile lifted her lips. "You always take such good care of me."

I certainly tried.

She gave me some of her dried sausage in return and fed me a cube of cheese, blissfully unaware of what she was doing to my poor heart. Especially when she accidentally grazed her fingers against my lips.

Moments like this made me wish it could be the two of us forever. No longer on the road but living together in a small house, somewhere in a valley where the sun shined plenty because it revealed the copper undertones in her dark hair, somewhere far away from anyone who knew she was my brother's window.

My daydream was interrupted by Mason's arrival who paused at our table. "Morning, girls. How's the food?"

"Delicious," I said earnestly, even if his presence set me on edge. The word felt foreign on my tongue even if I'd been taught the old language since I was a child.

"I'm glad to hear." He hesitated, his hand brushing through his beard. "Listen, I'm sorry about last night. Rudeus has told me many times where travellers have come from and where they're going is none of my business."

Konomi waved his apology away. "It's all right. We were just taken aback. We don't meet many people who know the sacred mountain. Have you ever been or...?"

I appreciated her gently probing for information. Whether she trusted these men or not, it was still strange that they knew exactly where we were from.

Mason chuckled gruffly. "Goodness, no. This old man isn't meant for travel. Bad back ever since I was a child. But we get travellers from all over. They bring the world to me with their wonderous stories of foreign lands and people. It's why I love tending to this old inn so much."

A strange feeling stirred in my stomach. "So you have met people from our region before?"

"Oh, I've met plenty of people from the west but you two aren't just travellers are you? I recognise the wolf emblems on your clothes and the hexagonal amulets around your neck. You're Guardians."

I froze, not that he noticed.

"You look familiar. Any chance you're related to, umm..." Mason looked over his shoulder. "Rudy! What was that last boy's name again? You know the one I'm talking about, from the sacred mountain?"

"Taka?" Rudeus shouted back.

"No, the other one!"

The other one? A chill ran down my spine. How many had there been?

Rudeus came to clear our plates away, slightly limping as he did. "Hanzo?"

"That's the one. Happy Hanzo," Mason said.

My throat constricted. Any doubts that he was telling the truth were erased by the name of my predecessor. Hanzo was the Guardian before me. I never knew he'd also gone on this sacred quest.

"No relation, but I met him once," I said, my voice coming out shaky.

"Did Hanzo tell you why he was here?" Konomi asked, the gentle way of her words disguising the shrewd curiosity underneath.

Mason settled at the table with us, taking his sweet time to get comfortable. He lit his pipe before he replied. "He said he was on some sort of quest to retrieve a sacred relic, just like all the previous Guardians."

My blood stilled in my veins and I caught Konomi's gaze, finding my doubts and worries reflected in her eyes. I didn't want to jump to conclusions but it very much sounded like the previous Guardian had been travelling east for the same reason as I was. If that was true, if he was on the same sacred quest, the Elders of the village never said anything. On the contrary, they'd made it sound like the Winter Stone being stolen was a recent thing.

I searched Mason's face for a hint of dishonesty but didn't find any in his blue eyes. I almost didn't dare ask my question, afraid to find out the answer, but I had to know. "How many Guardians have passed through here?"

A cloud of smoke escaped from his bearded mouth. "Hmm... I don't know exactly how many, but it started before I was born. I remember my first time, though I was only a boy when I met Kenji. He was a bit older than me, taller, very curious and kind. He was always talking about honour and his village, about some sacred quest he was on. I loved listening to him, that lovely accent of his. He was the person that made me understand what it was like to have butterflies in your stomach. He was only here for a week or so but I was absolutely smitten. I was heartbroken when he left but he said he would be back before winter was over. I waited years." Mason was silent for a bit and he wasn't looking at either of us, as if his memories were more vivid than what was happening in front of him. He released a few puffs of his pipe before he remembered he was telling a story.

"About seven years passed and I'd pretty much forgotten about Kenji. You know how infatuations come and go. It was winter again when a young woman arrived at our inn, not much older than yourself. She had the same raven-black hair and dark eyes. For one silly moment, I thought Kenji was back."

Konomi spoke, her voice thin. "It was another Guardian?"

"I don't remember her name, but she told me the same story as Kenji. About honour, and sacred quests, and her village. She was curious and kind too, but not Kenji. And she never came back either. There've been more. Sometimes they're alone, sometimes they're travelling with family. They come, they go, they never make it back despite their promises."

I studied the wrinkles on Mason's face, trying to estimate his age. His skin was weathered, like worn leather, and his beard was mostly grey. If he was a boy when the first Guardian came, the Elders would've been sending them for decades. It didn't make sense. Had our village been without the Winter Stone, and the Great Wolf's protection, all this time?

Konomi's touch startled me from my thoughts. "Mayu... Are you all right?"

I faked a smile. "Yes, I'm fine."

Mason's gaze flitted between Konomi and me. "I'm aware I don't know the full story and that it's not my place, but I have to say this. Coyote Country is no place for two young women. Don't continue east. Turn around, go back home. Whatever you're looking for can't be more important than your lives."

As heartfelt as his request was and as confusing as this situation had become, it didn't matter. Even if there'd been plenty of Guardians before me, this was my quest now. I had to succeed. The honour of my family and the safety of my village depended on it.

SIX

I brought the axe down, splitting a piece of wood perfectly in the middle with a dull thwack. I knew my father would be proud if he could see me. He taught me many years ago how to handle these chores. Mother never approved and would point out that it wasn't necessary, they had a son to rely on for these things.

Until they didn't.

With a grimace, I repeated the process, my mind drifting to the village and what was left of my family. I hoped my little brother was coping with his two older siblings gone. If it had been a choice, I would've stayed but the Elders were always very clear. Becoming the Guardian wasn't a choice, but an honour and duty. There'd been a whole ceremony and speech.

I couldn't help but wonder if they told my predecessors the exact same thing when they were forced to leave their families behind. All for the elusive Winter Stone. I didn't even know what it looked like or what it did except that it would let me shift into a real wolf. Although I wasn't sure if that was a myth or not.

The sound of footsteps made me look up. It was Konomi with refreshments and snacks, which she carried with great focus and concentration.

"Rudeus thought you might be a little hungry," she said, pausing a step away from me. She held out a plate of sausages and dried fruit.

Moments like this made me think of my older brother and what his life could've been like if he hadn't died. He would've been the luckiest man on earth to have a woman as warm and dutiful as her to tend to their home, but he would never have seen the wild side of her that ran into ice cold water without hesitation or climbed trees to steal eggs from nests. He would never have known that laugh of hers though, the one that was far too loud for a decent woman. Those were all parts of her I would never have known if we hadn't left the village, parts of her that I loved the most.

I pushed the thoughts away and wiped my hands on an old cloth before accepting the plate. "Thank you."

Her gaze went to the battlefield of logs. "He also said you've done plenty."

"Just a little more. Otherwise, I'll feel guilty for staying here so long," I said.

Konomi's smile touched her eyes. "You're always so diligent, Mayu. It's one of the things I admire most about you."

Her compliment made my cheeks even hotter than they already were. I didn't know what to say, so I just ate the dried sausage while I gave my muscles a rest. All the walking and hiking had been good to build stamina but the scarcity of food in the past weeks had taken a toll on my body.

I held the plate out to Konomi. "Do you want some?"

"No, thank you." She watched me with those curious eyes of hers. "You're not trying to get all this wood done today so we can sneak out without feeling guilty, right?"

Her question stunned me. Mostly because I had considered it.

I set the axe down, not even bothering to deny it. "You know me too well."

A triumphant smile lifted Konomi's lips, drawing my attention to them. They were red like ripe raspberries and I'd often wondered if they would taste like it too. I quickly pushed those thoughts to the back of my head and instead, brought them back to what was more important.

"I still think Mason and Rudeus are suspicious," I said as I gave the empty plate back to her. "All of this is suspicious."

"It's strange, I'll agree with you on that. I didn't know the Winter Stone had been missing for so long or that multiple Guardians have tried to retrieve it." Konomi kicked some of the logs to the side. "I suppose they could've been lying but they knew their names and details that nobody outside our village should know."

"Exactly. Suspicious."

She chuckled and it made my heart ache. To distract myself, I chopped more wood. That gave me something to do and somewhere to look that wasn't her beautiful face.

"I still think we should leave as soon as possible," I said between thuds of the axe.

Konomi let out a thoughtful hum. "I don't believe

that's wise. We should take this opportunity to rest, to hunt, and to talk to other travellers about the area. If we have better directions, we can avoid getting lost again."

I let the axe come down again. "You're right, I know you're right. I'm just uncomfortable. How many Guardians has the village sent on this quest? Did they really all pass through here? If that's true, how long has the Winter Stone been gone? Has the village been without protection this whole time?" I rattled off all my questions, bar one. *Why did nobody ever return?* I was too afraid of the answer.

"I want to know the same things." Konomi's gaze found mine. "I'm certain we will find all the answers eventually, but right now, our survival is more important than answers. Rest, food, preparations."

"If we're going to stay here longer, then I suppose it's a good thing I've cut so much wood," I said, picking the axe back up. Mother never approved of me learning these types of skills but there were other important things she taught me, like how to give more than to take. Even if I wasn't ready to trust Mason and Rudeus, I wasn't going to take advantage of their hospitality.

I cut more logs into pieces, only to realise that Konomi was watching my every move. I tried not to pay her attention but it was hard to ignore her. Especially when she was looking at me so intensely.

I lowered my axe. "You don't have to stay."

"I enjoy watching you. You're strong."

Her compliment stirred something in my chest but I ignored it. I cut a few more pieces but my focus was blown. I lowered the axe again. "I can't do it with you watching me. You make me nervous."

"Why?"

"I, just, because."

She took a step closer. "Can I try?"

"Try what?" I followed her gaze to the axe. "You want to chop some wood?"

Konomi nodded, only a small step away. Her hand landed on my wrist, her touch featherlight but deliberate at the same time. She looked up in my eyes, the sun making hers sparkle. "I want to be able to do this too. You should teach me."

My stomach twisted into knots from having her so close and I could feel my traitorous gaze flit down to her lips. It would only take one move to bridge the distance but I could never, no matter how much I wanted to. She could never know how much I was yearning for her touch, how I wanted her in ways that would make her ears burn if she could hear me thoughts.

I swallowed my desire away, bringing the axe in between us. "Sure, I can teach you. Here. Grip the end with both hands. Spread your legs slightly, you want to make sure you have a good stance." My cheeks flared hot as I relayed innocent instructions that suddenly didn't sound all that innocent. This was supposed to help me not think about her.

Konomi bounced slightly, testing her foothold. "Okay, now what?"

Without looking at her, I put a log on the cutting stump. "Aim at the middle, but don't force it. You don't want to lose control. It's better to do it gently at first."

"Oh, I'll be gentle," Konomi promised.

The heat in my stomach sank to my lower belly. If only she knew what she was doing to me, would she be disgusted with me? Upset? No, that wasn't Konomi. Knowing her, she would likely feel sad for me that I had these feelings that she couldn't return. She would be gentle with me and that somehow made it even worse.

SEVEN

Time at the Red Boar Inn passed slowly. Konomi made herself familiar with the kitchen, much to Rudeus' delight and praise. When she wasn't helping him, she chopped wood like she'd been doing it her whole life while I set traps all around the inn. The rabbits and pheasants were lean during winter but also desperate, making them easy to catch.

I still didn't know if we could trust the two old men running the inn but staying had been the right choice. Especially when the snow came.

The front door of the inn shrieked open and Konomi came in, snow resting on her shoulders and her dark hair. Her cheeks were flushed pink from the cold, a look I particularly adored on her.

She gave her basket with foraged goods to

Rudeus who looked at her like she was some sort of goddess. I understood how he felt. Only Konomi could go into a winter forest and emerge with a bounty, a skill that had saved me and my shaky fingers many times during our journey.

Our eyes met and I quickly averted my gaze, embarrassed to be caught staring. I turned my attention back on the shoe I was fortifying, pretending like I'd been doing that all along. She approached me from behind, not nearly as subtle as she thought she was. Or maybe she didn't mean to be.

Her little giggle gave her away and without even a greeting, she pressed her ice cold hands against my cheeks. I gasped as the sensation made me shiver in a way that had nothing to do with the coldness and everything feeling her pressed against my back.

I squirmed out of her touch, laughing from the nervous energy coursing through me. She didn't relent and pushed one hand down the back of my neck.

"Konomi!" I shouted, twisting to get away from her and somehow twisting into her. Her whole face was lit up with childlike glee and that innocence made me feel even more guilty about the flashes of desire sparking through me.

"It's cold outside," she said redundantly, still grinning.

"I can tell."

"It's absolutely gorgeous, too. The sky is the most beautiful blue and the snow glitters like it's covered with crystals. You should come see."

"Why would I go outside when I don't have to?"

Konomi folded her hands together. "Pleeeeeaase. It'll be fun, I promise."

If only I was capable of saying no to her. I abandoned my repairs and followed her outside, fully intending to have just a look. I didn't even put on my coat because while there was something to be said for appreciating nature and the wonders of winter, I much preferred the warmth and safety of the inn. In fact, if I'd known this journey was going to be this cold and miserable, I might've never gone in the first place.

The fresh snow was truly as beautiful as she described but it paled in comparison with the smile on Konomi's face. She ran through the snow, leaving a trail of tracks that seemed to delight her like she was a child seeing its first winter.

"Come on!" she shouted, waving for me to join her.

"Don't even think about it," I called back, staying

right by the inn. Despite the snow, it wasn't all that cold. There was no cold breeze or chill in the air, just a crisp dry winter's day.

Konomi grinned as she collected a handful of snow. She balled it together and held it up with an impish grin.

"Don't you dare," I warned her.

The snowball came flying my way, missing me by a hair. It hit the inn with a dull thud instead and was followed by a carefree laugh from Konomi that made some nearby birds scatter. Just seeing her so unburdened and happy made me feel warm and giddy. There was something so irresistible about her unbridled ability to have fun, I had no choice but to give in.

I reached down to form a snowball of my own and threw it her way, hitting her in the stomach with the practised aim of an archer. She squealed in delight, clearly pleased she roped me into her little game, and fired more back. Her aim was surprisingly good and even though I ran away, one of them hit my face. The cold burst made my skin tingle and glow like it was held near a fire.

Konomi's concerned laughter clattered through the air. "I'm so sorry! Are you okay?"

Instead of replying or wasting more time

throwing snow her way, I charged directly at her. She only understood my intention when I was mere steps away and by then, it was too late. I threw myself onto her, knocking her to the ground. Our fall was cushioned by the snow and her laugh mingled with my own.

I grabbed a handful of snow and let it rain on her face as payback, trying to ignore just how beautiful her dark hair was sprawled out in the white tapestry of snow. She wriggled in protest, somehow managing to throw me off. Without wasting a moment, she jumped on me and pinned me underneath her with surprising ease.

I bucked to free myself, only pressing myself more into her as she pinned me down. My laughter ebbed away as I became aware of different sensations. The feel of her cold hands enclosed around my wrists, her strong thighs straddled around me. Her face was surprisingly close to mine, so close I could feel her warm breath on my lips.

"Konomi," I managed, surprising both her and me with how strangled I sounded. Without meaning to, I imagined her cold lips on mine, her hands travelling down where the heat of me would warm them up.

She let go of my wrists but remained on top, her look pensive like she was on the verge of working something out. Panic lashed through me and I shoved her, harder than necessary. She tumbled backwards and I scrambled out from underneath her, panting like I'd just ran a mile.

"Sorry," I murmured, although I wasn't entirely sure what I was apologising for. Knocking her to the ground or the indecent thoughts running through my head.

"It's fine," she said, not quite sounding like herself.

"We should go back inside," I said, avoiding looking her in the eyes, too afraid of what she would see in mine.

"Mayu—"

I ignored her and fled to the inn, my poor heart hammering in my chest with such force, I was afraid it would break. The longer this kept going on, the more I was sure it inevitably would.

EIGHT

Despite my worries, Konomi seemed none the wiser about my feelings and it was easy to fall back into the routine of our life. While we helped out at the inn, we prepared for the next leg of our journey. We chatted to the owners of the inn, gathered information about the surroundings, planned our next route, and mended our tools and belongings as we waited for the worst of the storm to pass.

Living here was nice. Rudy and Mason were great hosts and excellent company now that I stopped worrying about them killing us in our sleep. When we left, I would miss this place. It was a peaceful existence, one that made me yearn with every fibre of my being for something that could never be. A home with Konomi.

As lovely as that feeling was, the longer it went on, the more it started feeling like a suffocating noose. It made me eager to get out of here and back out in the wild where those foolish notions didn't have as strong of a hold on me.

One particular afternoon, I was sitting at one of the long tables in the main room. The fire was crackling happily in the hearth, untended since the owners were out. They'd left the inn in our hands, or rather, Konomi's hands. In the short time we'd been here, both of them had taken a shine to her, something I could easily understand.

Konomi came in with a basket of wood, setting it down next to me. "What do you think?"

All the pieces were cleanly cut and uniform in size. It was so like her to do everything with the same diligence and care. No half measures, no excuses, just practice and effort.

"Perfect," I said.

She beamed. "Thank you. Now I can help you with this when we're travelling again. Or protect me from a robber."

I felt myself smile. "So are you going to be sleeping with an axe under your pillow instead of your knife?"

Konomi trailed her fingers up the handle of the

axe. "Hmmm... No, this is a bit too bulky. I'll stick with my trusted dagger. If someone tried to overwhelm me while I'm asleep, it would just take one swoosh, and I'd have the blade against their throat."

I involuntarily reached up to my neck and swallowed hard. I was sure that warning wasn't meant for me but that made me feel even worse. She trusted me and I was betraying her constantly with my traitorous thoughts and desires.

Eager to change the subject, I turned my attention back to the map. It wasn't much, just a piece of old parchment with some vague descriptions and markers that should help us find the nearest village. It was only three days away but the path took us through a narrow mountain pass that was known for cougar attacks.

Konomi leaned down to look at the map, bringing herself closer to me. I could smell the light musk of her underneath the hint of soap and I wanted to bury my nose into her neck. Instead, I shuffled away which she took as an invitation to sit down.

"There are cats living in the mountains?" She tapped on the spot marked with a small drawing of a cougar.

"Cougars," I clarified.

She chuckled. "Oh, that makes more sense. Your drawing doesn't make them look very dangerous though."

"It got fangs and claws," I pointed out, although she was right. My drawing skills were limited to trees and mountains and houses, the normal things to put down on a map.

"I see it now." She nudged her shoulder against mine. "How far are we from Coyote Country, do you think?"

I grabbed another map. "We're supposed to be a little over halfway. It'll depend on the weather if that's true."

Konomi was silent for a bit. "And when we get there. What then?"

Her answer sparked the first hints of anxiety within me. I'd asked the Elders that exact same question but they'd only offered me vague reassurances about how my wolf soul would guide me to the Winter Stone. How as the Guardian, I would be able to sense its presence.

Back then, I had no choice but to believe them. Now? Now the situation was different. I knew more, I'd seen more. I was weary from the trip, scared about the unknown, more suspicious and less trusting. But I wasn't sure if I was ready to let go of the Elders' word because without it, this whole thing was a fool's quest and a lost cause.

I looked at Konomi, my gut stirring with turmoil. There were things I could lie about, like my feelings, and things I couldn't. Like this.

"I don't know," I told her truthfully. "As the Guardian, they said I would be able to sense the presence of the Stone. But how long it'll take, I'm not sure. I'm not sure about anything."

She nodded slowly. "Sounds like we have a long journey ahead of us."

"We do. Well, I do. You..." I almost didn't dare say it, afraid that saying the words out loud would be giving them power. "You don't have to come all the way with me. It's *my* duty, I'm the Guardian. You're free to go wherever your heart desires."

She gave me a blank look. "What does that mean? What are you trying to say?"

"Nothing, just that you're not bound to this quest. Or to me." I almost choked on the last bit but it was true. The Elders appointed me, it was my life that had been signed away. She didn't have to be here, she didn't have to make this sacrifice.

Her eyes darkened. "Is that what you think? That I would just abandon you because it's hard or perilous? I knew that would be the case when I decided to go with you."

"You couldn't have imagined it would be like this, though. I didn't know it would be like this. This hard, this long, this lonely, " I said quietly, not sure why I'd chosen today to say the things I'd been worrying about the entire time.

Behind us, one of the logs settled and the fire spat embers in the air that fizzled out with a soft crinkle.

Konomi took my hand in hers, squeezing it fiercely. "Listen to me carefully, Mayu. You didn't have any choice in becoming the Guardian or accepting this quest, but I did. I chose this. I chose to come on this journey. I chose *you.*"

My stomach clenched at the intensity of her words. It almost sounded like a confession. My desperate heart wanted it to be.

"Why *did* you come with me?" I whispered.

"Because." Konomi took a shaky breath. "You're my dearest friend, my sister-in-law. Travelling alone is far too dangerous. And it's not like I had a real reason to stay in the village."

I'd asked her plenty of times before and she'd given this answer plenty of times before. It never fully satisfied me. I didn't know whether it was because I didn't believe her or I didn't want to. Could she really have come along for those simple reasons?

Maybe I simply couldn't imagine doing all this for a friend. Maybe I was just a much worse person than her.

Konomi's eyes locked with mine. "Why are you talking about all this? Is this your way of saying you want me to leave?"

"No!" I instinctively reached for her hands, grasping them tightly like she could disappear at any moment. "By the Great Wolf, no, I don't want you to leave. Never."

It was the honest truth. As hard as it could be to repress my feelings, life without Konomi would be so much worse. I didn't even want to think about what I would do without her. She was my everything.

A smile lifted Konomi's lips but it didn't fully reach her eyes. She twisted her hands up so we were holding each other instead of me grasping at her. "Good, because I don't want to leave. I've always wanted to see the world and now I'm getting the chance. I like trying all this new food and meeting different people."

"Of course, you do. You're good with people." It was true, no matter where we went, people always instantly took to her. They usually took a moment longer to accept me but I didn't blame them, I was a bit more distant and gruffer than sweet and bubbly Konomi.

Konomi squeezed my hands. "You've got lots of good qualities too. You always know what to do, where to go. You're reliable, strong, decisive. Brave. You're so good at archery, I could never hit a target, let alone a moving one."

Heat made my ears tingle and I felt uncharacteristically shy. I cast my gaze down, unable to look her in the eyes as I demanded more. "Say more nice things about me."

A light chuckle left Konomi's mouth. "You're kind, funny, thoughtful, and good-looking too."

I looked at her, snickering. "Okay, now you're exaggerating."

"I'm not." She sucked in her bottom lip. "You have the most beautiful eyes."

"I do?" I asked, my voice barely more than a whisper. I suddenly felt very shy but warm too. Getting such heartfelt compliments from Konomi was making my heart clench.

She nodded. "They're really lovely and dark and they curl when you smile."

My lips lifted from her comment.

Konomi smiled too. "See, like that. I love it when you smile."

"Me too, I love your smile," I said, my heart pounding. I just felt so warm and whole and I wanted to hold her hands forever. "When I see your smile, it's like the sun comes up. You're the most beautiful person I've ever met, I could look at you forever." The words slipped from my tongue before I fully realised what exactly I'd just confessed.

"Oh, Mayu. I—" She looked pained for a moment, like she wanted to say something but didn't know how.

I was an idiot, I said too much, far too much.

Rudy and Mason chose that time to stomp into the inn with lots of ruckus and laughter. Their sudden presence was jarring and I didn't know who dropped their hands first, me or Konomi. It didn't matter. The moment, if it could even be called that, was over.

Konomi looked suspiciously red as she moved back. It was only a small step but it hurt.

"I should go see if they need my help," she said, turning away.

"Konomi." I surprised myself how desperate I sounded, like I was begging her for something she could never know.

She ignored me, something she rarely did, and practically fled, clearly desperate to get away.

Her rejection stung but mostly, I was angry at myself for being so desperate for her affection. I'd clearly freaked her out with my confession. I was such an idiot.

I was going to ruin everything if I didn't get a hold of myself.

NINE

Despite being stuck in one small inn together, Konomi managed to avoid me for the rest of the day. During dinner, she was almost her usual self but not quite. I didn't know how exactly I could tell but there was just a slight difference in her smile, the pitch of her voice, the eye contact she seemed to avoid. She was pretending everything was fine which meant it wasn't.

Later, when I went up to our room to sleep, Konomi didn't come with me. Instead, she claimed she was going to help Rudy with something in the kitchen. One of her eyes twitched when she lied, a sure-fire tell.

I went up to the room by myself, cursing myself for causing this fracture. I was almost changed into my night robe when a knock sounded on the bedroom door.

"Can I come in?" Konomi asked from the other side.

She'd never knocked before, or asked permission to enter. It just underlined that something was seriously wrong between us.

"Just a moment," I shouted back, like she hadn't seen me undressed hundreds of times. But for some reason, I really didn't want her to see me like that right now. I already felt vulnerable and bare enough.

Once I was fully changed and hidden under the covers, I called to say that she could come in. I didn't like that things were changing between us but that was my price to pay for not keeping a good handle on my wretched feelings.

The door creaked and Konomi entered with careful steps. She looked surprised to see me in bed already and seemed a bit lost all of a sudden. She remained in the middle of the room, sort of turned towards me. "About earlier. What you said..."

I tensed as memories from earlier came flooding back, my mistake with which I almost revealed everything. "Forget what I said."

"What? But—"

"Please. I don't want to talk about earlier. *Ever.*" I

bit the inside of my cheek, afraid that if she would ask me about my feelings now, I wouldn't manage to hide them.

Konomi took a step closer to my bed. "But I thought—"

"Please!" I insisted, too scared to even look at her in case she could see these secret feelings in my eyes.

A beat of tense silence passed followed by a sigh. "I'll just get ready for bed."

As usual, I turned away from her to give her some privacy. That didn't stop my mind from conjuring images that accompanied the rustling sounds of her clothes being taken off. I squeezed my eyes shut as if that somehow would help but it never did.

My cheeks were on fire by the time I heard the creak of her bed and I could finally breathe again.

Outside, it was hailing. I could hear the monotonous staccato clattering as it hit the ground and turned the fresh snow even more dangerous to thread. There would be no travelling tomorrow either which was infuriating. The last place I wanted to be right now was trapped in an inn with Konomi.

She broke the awkward silence in the room. "I've been thinking..."

My throat closed. "About?"

"About your parents. They were always so kind to me, especially your mother since I didn't have one of my own. That was my favourite thing about being married to your brother, being a part of your family."

Her words gripped my heart and constricted around it like a snake killing its prey. She had no idea how much it killed me to hear this, how close I was to being reduced to sobs. Or maybe she did and this was her way of putting me in my place, of reminding me what we were to each other.

Her sheets rustled. "Mayu?"

I briefly considered pretending to be asleep but maybe it would be good to hear this. Maybe being cut down was what my heart needed so I could move on.

"Yes?" I whispered, ever so grateful for the dark.

"When we return with the Winter Stone, what do you think our lives will be like?"

I bit my lip. "I don't know. The Guardian is meant to be a position of honour. I believe I would be in charge of protecting the village. I suppose I would live in that nice house on the hill near the temple while I protect the village."

Konomi let out a weird breath. "Do you think... do you think you would live there alone?"

My hands tightened into fists. "I don't know.

Unmarried women don't usually leave their parents' house but I don't know if that rule would apply to me as a Guardian. I'm not even sure if it's a rule or just tradition."

"There's Old Lady Mu who lives by herself near the river. She never married."

I swallowed hard. "That's true. I'm not really in a rush to get married so I suppose I would live there by myself."

"What about me?" Konomi asked, her voice strangely close even though she was far away. Maybe it was just the hushed tone, barely louder than a breath.

My throat constricted and I forced the words out, desperately trying to sound casual but I didn't know if I managed. The blood was rushing through my ears so loudly, I couldn't hear my own voice. "You're a widow, things are different for you. You can do whatever you want. You could even remarry if you wished."

"What if I wanted to live with you instead?"

This time, my heart actually stopped. "What?"

"Nobody would find that strange. We're friends, really good friends. We're family. And we know we enjoy each other's company." She faltered. "Unless you don't want to live with me."

"No, it's not that. I would. It's just..." I so wanted to say yes but my conscience wouldn't let me. "I'm not sure it would be fair."

"Fair? To whom? Your parents? I'm sure they won't mind."

I swallowed hard. "To you."

"To me? Why?" Konomi's voice was ever so slightly croaky.

This would've been a good time to tell her, to confess those feelings I'd secretly harboured even before she married my brother. The words were on my tongue, my heart pounding in my chest. It was dark, dark enough that she wouldn't be able to see my face or my tears.

But I couldn't.

"We should go to sleep," I said instead.

"Mayu. Why wouldn't it be fair?" It was rare for Konomi to be so persistent.

It made me hate myself that I couldn't give her an answer. She didn't deserve to be deceived which was exactly why we couldn't live together. It would all be a grand deception, one that only got bigger as more time went on.

I turned on my side, away from her. "Can you please let it go?"

Konomi didn't answer and eventually her

breathing grew steady which meant she'd fallen asleep.

That was how close we were. I could tell when she was sleeping simply from listening to her. It felt like something very intimate.

I wondered if my older brother had been able to tell too and that thought pierced through my heart like an arrow. Of course he'd known, they were married. He would know all this about Konomi and more, like how it felt to be caressed by her fingers, the taste of her lips. All sorts of things I didn't know and would never find out.

TEN

After a restless night of tossing and turning, I felt absolutely horrible. This was worse than a hangover, worse than when I fell from a tree as a child after being warned not to climb it. And to make matters worse, Konomi was gone from her bed when I woke up.

For one traitorous moment, I thought she'd abandoned me.

I didn't feel relieved when I found her eating breakfast at the long table, just more guilty that I'd doubted her impeccable character. She was far too kind and honourable to do something nasty like disappearing in the night.

That was something I would do.

"Morning," I muttered as I sat opposite her. We were the only guests here which offered privacy, but I didn't know if that was a good thing or not.

Konomi cleared her throat. "Good morning, Mayu."

"H-How did you sleep?" I still didn't manage to look her in the eye. I shouldn't have worried because she didn't seem to want to look at me either.

"Perfectly well, thank you." She sounded so formal and distant, it was blood-chilling.

Rudy came from the kitchen with a bowl of porridge for my breakfast and set it down, not picking up on the strange tension between us. He chattered happily about something but I didn't hear a word of it. I was too focused trying to decipher Konomi's blank expression.

I managed two bites of the lukewarm oat mush before I realised I couldn't take another bite with this energy.

"What's wrong?" I asked, not sure if I was ready to hear what was wrong but I couldn't stop myself. I'd never had all that good a grip on myself, or I'd have managed to kill my feelings for her a long time ago.

"Nothing." She was a terrible liar.

I put my spoon down. "Konomi."

"Let it go," she said, using my own words against me.

"No." I knew it was unfair not to give her the same grace as she afforded me. But then, if I was a better person, none of this would be happening. This whole thing was unfair. Of all the people I could be in love with, why did it have to be with the one person who I couldn't escape, the one person who didn't feel the same?

Konomi's gaze snapped up to mine, her voice colder than I'd ever heard it. "Really? You're going to be like that?"

Guilt lashed through me and I suddenly felt deeply ashamed of my behaviour. I got up, unable to be in her presence any longer. I had no right behaving like this. She wasn't to blame for this hurt, it was all me.

"Why don't you want to live with me?" Konomi's jaw was tensed, like it pained her to even ask the question.

It took me a moment to process the situation. This was what she was upset about?

I settled back at the table, my mind racing to come up with acceptable answers that wouldn't reveal my crush or hurt her feelings. We were close, good friends, technically family. There was no good reason why we couldn't share a house, none apart from my poor heart.

"It's not that I don't want to live with you," I said slowly, not sure where I was going with it. I just knew I couldn't sit here and let her stay upset. I needed a simple explanation, something that made sense.

"Then what?" Konomi asked.

"I'm... I'm afraid." That was not a lie. "Afraid we won't find the Winter Stone and there will be no returning home for us."

"Oh." Konomi's eyes locked with mine. "That's it?"

I hummed affirmingly, not able to get the actual lie over my lips.

She let out a breath. "I'm sorry, but I don't believe you. There's something else going on. You've been acting weird lately. Skittish. Distant. Is it... because of me?"

Panic gripped my heart. *She knew*.

She rubbed her temples with a panicked look. "I knew it. I knew I wasn't making it up. You've been avoiding my gaze, shying away from my touch. You can't even look at me right now." She looked like she could cry. "I knew it. You're—"

"Yes, I'm in love with you!" I interrupted, the words exploding from me. I almost felt relieved, like the very brief moment of free fall before the noose tightens. "I know, it's wrong. You're my brother's wife, my best friend. I've been lying to you for so long, it's horrible. I wish I didn't feel like this, I tried not to show it, I tried to get over it but you're always here, always so close."

Konomi looked shocked to her core, her eyes larger than I'd ever seen them. "Y-You love me? What? How? Since *when*?"

Her surprise confused me. Why was she acting like this confession was completely out of the blue? The way she'd been talking, it was clear she knew.

My stomach dropped. What if she didn't know and I'd just blurted all this out?

I clasped my hands over my mouth, horrified at what I'd just said. At what I'd just done.

"Mayu—"

Bile pushed up to the back of my throat and I scrambled up from the table, blind to where I was going. I ran into a chair on my way out, deaf to Konomi shouting my name after her. I threw the front door of the inn open, temporarily blinded by the harsh sunlight. There was another layer of fresh snow outside but I ruined it without a second thought, running through it like a rabbit escaping from an arrow.

I didn't know where I was going, I just needed to get away. And because I was so much more awful than Konomi, I genuinely thought of not coming back.

ELEVEN

It was dark when I finally returned to the inn with my metaphorical tail between my legs. It wasn't by choice, I just had nowhere else to go. For a moment, I feared the front door would be locked and all my stuff kicked out but that wasn't the case.

I pushed inside as quietly as I could, relieved to find the main room empty. The fire in the hearth was reduced to a smoulder and the warmth embraced me like a long lost child. I was so cold, I wanted to crawl into the coals and burn. Instead, I tiptoed upstairs, praying that Konomi was already asleep.

The door creaked so loudly, I was sure the entire inn heard it. I paused on the threshold, listening for Konomi's breathing. It sounded even and deep which meant she was asleep.

I closed the door, begging it to be silent, but failing. Everything was so much louder when I was trying to be quiet. My shoes thudded on the floor when I took them off despite me setting them down slowly. I changed into my night robe and the bedsheets sounded as loud as a nearby storm when I slipped into bed. It creaked too, like it was on the verge of collapsing.

Even my heartbeat felt so strong, I was sure it could be heard outside my body.

I nestled my head down on my pillow, trying to temper my breathing. Despite being outside for a whole day on my own, I still hadn't come up with a solution. I supposed there was none. We just had to carry on like normal because splitting up would be a death sentence. My feelings were irrelevant, I had a sacred quest resting on my shoulders. It was the only thing that mattered. Although the further I got away from the village and the Elders, the less I cared.

A sound came from Konomi's side and her breathing changed. "You're back."

I almost couldn't breathe. "You're awake? Why didn't you say anything?" I'd been so sure she was asleep, maybe I didn't know her as well as I thought.

"Because I didn't want you to run away again.

I've been so worried about you. Are you all right? Are you hurt?"

"I'm fine, just cold." I swallowed the guilt away. "I'm sorry, I shouldn't have worried you."

Her bed creaked and I heard the sound of her bare feet hitting the wooden floor. It only took her two steps to get to my bed and I froze even more than I already was, afraid of what was about to happen. If she wanted to slap me, I deserved it.

Instead, she slipped under the covers with me. The warmth of her body was almost painful but oh so welcome.

She gasped. "Mayu! You're freezing."

I mustered a weak smile. "It's cold outside."

"You fool. You're such a fool." She grasped my arm, her fingers almost painfully digging into my skin. "I'm so glad you're back."

The guilt was unbearable. "I won't worry you like that again, I promise."

"You better not," she whispered.

Something warm pressed against my cheek and it took me a moment to realise it was her lips. My heart fluttered like it was going to explode. I didn't know what I'd done to warrant such tenderness and grace from her but I definitely didn't deserve it.

Her warm fingers slid up to my chin and she

turned my head so I was looking at her. We were sharing my pillow so her face was only inches away and the full moon meant I could see every detail of her. The slight slope of her rounded nose, the lift of her cheeks, the fullness of her lips. She was so beautiful it ached.

Konomi swallowed visibly. "Earlier today... I wanted to talk to you because I was worried that I'd been too forward."

"What do you mean?" I breathed, not sure what she was talking about.

"I was so sure that you'd realised... how *I* felt about you. That you were pulling away because you were disgusted with me."

Hope bloomed up within me together with confusion. I didn't know why she was saying these things, maybe it was all a delusion caused by the frost, but I didn't care. I so desperately wanted to hear these words, even if it was only a dream.

"What do you mean?" I wetted my lips. "How do you feel about me?"

"I love you, Mayu. I'm *in* love with you. I have been for a while now. That's what I wanted to tell you before you confessed and stormed out."

This had to be a fever dream but it was beautiful and everything I'd ever wanted. I shuffled closer, bridging the space on the pillow so I could press my lips against hers. They burned against mine and didn't taste of raspberries but of something much sweeter.

Konomi let out a strangled breath as she kissed me back. She was gentle and soft until she wasn't, until her lips became harder and more insistent. She opened her mouth and her warm tongue touched mine, causing me to jolt back.

"Too much?" she asked, panting slightly.

"This is real." I touched my lips, as if I would find the answer on them.

Konomi frowned. "Of course, this is real?"

I grasped her arm, harder than necessary but she didn't seem to mind the touch. Instead, she melted more into me, the heat of her body making mine tingle. This was real. Konomi felt the same way. She didn't just accept my feelings, she loved me. She *loved* me.

A strangled sob welled up from the depths of me and Konomi's arms tightened around me.

"Are you all right? I'm sorry, was this too much?"

"No, this was perfect. I'm just overwhelmed. I didn't think this was real, I didn't believe this could ever happen. I love you, Konomi. I love you, I love you, *I love you.*"

She chuckled warmly and patted the top of my head affectionately. "There, there. If you want to cry, I'll hold you."

I snuggled deeper into her, my face pressed into the crook of her neck. She smelled even more like herself there and I wanted her scent more than air. She shifted ever so slightly to the side and the movement made me suddenly very aware of the rest of her body, of her leg pressing between mine.

A different tingle danced up my spine and I kissed her again, searching for that same jolt of pleasure. I searched for her tongue with mine, groaning when she parted her lips for me. She kissed me deeply, hungrily, with a fierceness that I wasn't used to from her. Almost like she wasn't in full control of herself and I loved that I was the cause of it.

Heat pooled in my stomach, gradually sinking lower until I could feel it between my legs. Until it was almost unbearable and I wanted to feel more of her.

Konomi sighed as she kissed down my neck. I never realised my skin was so sensitive there but with every kiss, a jolt of pleasure shot straight down to my core. I didn't know it could feel like this but I wanted more, so much more.

"You're so warm," I breathed between our kisses

as I let my hands graze up and down her back. I didn't dare touch more, afraid that she wasn't the only one with uncontrollable desires.

"And you're terribly cold." Her fingers wandered down my chest, resting on my stomach. "Are you cold everywhere?"

I took a sharp breath in, hoping she was thinking of the same thing as me. "I am. So very cold."

"Would you like me to warm you up?" she whispered, her voice tickling the shell of my ear.

My answer came out husky. "Yes."

Her fingers pressed into my skin. "Where?"

"Everywhere," I breathed.

Her hand slipped further down, over my hip bone, down to my thigh where my night robe ended. The first touch of her fingers on my skin made me shiver in the best way possible and my body tensed in anticipation.

"Tell me if you want to stop," Konomi said, her hand paused on my bare leg.

"Don't stop." I sounded as eager as I felt. It was almost pathetic but I didn't care. I just wanted her.

She helped me out of my robe and I shivered from the sudden brush of cold air, but not for long. Konomi's warm hands were instantly back on my skin followed by her burning lips. I'd never been kissed like that by anyone but it didn't feel foreign or strange, just right. She touched and caressed, soft in the right places, insistent in others.

I rolled onto my back and she straddled me, the inside of her thighs warm against my hips. There was a different heat there too, one that made me excited to feel it against me. She smiled, an elusive smile, and crossed her arms to pull her night robe over her head. My breath hitched as she exposed herself in a way she'd never done, with an invitation to look, marvel, admire.

I'd dreamt and fantasised so much about this but now that it was happening, I couldn't move my hands. I was too afraid that touching her would somehow snap her out of this spell.

She ran her hands down her body, slowly, teasingly, lingering as she cupped her breasts.

I was mesmerised.

She touched her nipple and I felt her thighs tighten around me. Something about the pressure snapped me from my stupor and I reached up, trailing my fingers along the same path as Konomi's. She gasped when I brushed them against her nipple and she squirmed a little more. I never knew my touch could do that to her and I grew bolder, eager to explore her body more.

The softest of gasps fell from her lips and I felt it right between my legs. Heat pooled where she was straddling me and flowed right to my core. My body was practically on fire by the time her hand finally slipped down my stomach again. She paused briefly and even though I'd never done this before, I knew exactly what I wanted. Where I wanted her touch.

I kissed her with open mouth, greedily, until her hand finally slipped between my legs. I arched into her, moaning as her touch caused a spark of pleasure that I'd only ever felt on the rare times I explored my own body.

I whimpered. "Do that again. Do more."

The moonlight framed Konomi's smile as she pressed her fingers into me, causing the heat between my legs to spread throughout my entire body. With every kiss, every brush of her fingers, the heat grew until it was unbearably wonderful. My nose was buried in her neck, her scent so overwhelmingly strong. I moaned as I lost control. My teeth sank into her skin and she held me the whole time while I rode out the sudden waves of pleasure.

A strange tug in my chest made me aware of my wolf soul and in that moment, I knew I'd never love anyone as much as her.

TWELVE

Morning came too quickly but it was warm and my whole bed smelled of Konomi. We'd fallen asleep with our arms and legs tangled, entwined like two branches of ivy growing together. I didn't ever want to be separated.

She stirred in her sleep, her eyes fluttering open slowly. Her eyelashes were short and so cute, I just wanted to kiss them. I wanted to kiss all of her.

"Good morning," I whispered. Our faces were so close, our noses were almost touching. It was still dark outside but after kissing and touching every inch of her, I didn't need light to see her anymore.

She smiled. "Morning, Mayu."

Her voice was slightly raspy in a way I'd never

heard before but it was my new favourite sound. That and her moans from last night.

I kissed her nose and then her lips. She moaned softly and kissed me back. The fire and urgency from last night was gone but the tenderness and intimacy wasn't.

"Any regrets?" she asked, her breath slightly hitching.

I shook my head slightly. "None. You?"

"Me either." She propped her head up with her hand, exposing the side of her neck that I bit last night without meaning to. It was slightly swollen and redder than the other marks my lips left.

"I hurt you," I whispered, reaching out to brush my fingers over the bite mark.

Konomi tilted her head back slightly. "It doesn't hurt."

"I'm still sorry. I don't know what came over me," I said, leaning in to kiss it better. She giggled and squirmed into me, which I took as encouragement to keep kissing and nibbling. She was just so irresistible and this was better than my dreams. This was real.

"I'm guessing I'm allowed to live in your fancy house on the hill now?" Konomi quipped, her voice slightly hoarse and husky again.

Her joke made my stomach tighten and I jerked

back. The movement cut through us like a blade, tearing the beautiful moment apart.

"Mayu?" Concern coloured Konomi's voice. "What's wrong?"

"N-Nothing. It's just... The house, the hill, the village. My family." I almost didn't manage the next word. *"My brother."*

Konomi touched my face. "It's all right. I knew this would be an issue, it's one of the many reasons why I never said anything. Why I never thought we could be... this."

"I feel so guilty, like I just betrayed... *him*. Do you not feel that way?" I whispered, afraid that if I said his name, he would come back from the afterlife to haunt me. Maybe he already was. I betrayed him, his memory.

"I do feel conflicted but not guilty." She was silent for a bit. "I think you loved him more than I did. I know that sounds awful but he was your beloved big brother. Whereas to me, he was—"

"Your husband." I felt nauseous just saying the word.

"A stranger. At least, at first." Konomi turned on her back but she never let go of my hand. "I liked him and I'm sure I would've grown to love him eventually.

But I don't think I would've ever loved him the way I love you."

My stomach tightened again but it felt different this time. This time, I felt betrayed on my brother's behalf. How could she say these things?

Konomi let out a sigh from deep within. "I've never told anyone this. I mean, there's nobody I could tell. I didn't really understand how I felt about you back then. I didn't even have much say in the marriage agreement. My father arranged it because he was dying and I didn't have a good reason to say no. Reasons, yes. Plenty of them. Good ones, no."

I squeezed her hand. "I'm sorry. I didn't know. I thought you wanted to marry him."

"I wanted to stay close to you." She turned to look at me even though it was still dark. "This was the only way I knew how. I am truly sorry. To you and to your brother. I never meant to deceive and yet, I did it to both of you. And the worst part is that I never regretted it because I got to spend more time with you. If I hadn't married him, I would never have been able to come on this journey with you. I was grateful that I could. How awful is that? I'm despicable."

"Oh, Konomi. No, you're not." I let go of her hand and she sobbed, clearly thinking I was moving away. Instead, I pulled her into a hug. It was odd to be the one embracing her, I was the younger one and she was my rock, but right now, I could tell she needed me to hold her. Just how she held me last night.

I stroked her hair while she clutched me so tightly, it almost hurt. I didn't mind, it felt good to acknowledge this hauntingly painful thing that had both bound and separated us for so long. It was healing to realise that life hadn't just felt unfair to me, but that it had been equally unfair to all of us. To me, to Konomi, to my brother.

After a while, Konomi stopped crying but she never let go. I kissed her forehead, her eyelids with those cute short eyelashes, her cheeks that were still wet from her tears. There was no way to change the past and no point in agonising over it. I didn't hate myself or Konomi enough to punish us over it either. My brother would never be fully gone from our relationship because I would carry him in my heart wherever we went, but he didn't have to stand between us either.

"So what do we do now?" Konomi asked in a small voice.

"We continue as planned. We have a Winter Stone to find," I said. I even managed to sound a little bit optimistic. "If we find it, we'll be hailed as heroes when we return. You and I will live in that fancy house. Together. Nobody will tell us we can't, I am *the* Guardian. Aren't I?"

Hope sparked in Konomi's beautiful eyes. "And if we don't find the Stone?"

"Then I suppose we'll have to find a different house on a different hill." I leaned forward, capturing her lips in another kiss. "If that's not what you want, then I'll do my very best to put these feelings back but I'm not sure I'll be able to. I'm greedy. I've spent so long wanting this, now that I've had a taste of you, I want everything."

My statement brought the first proper smile back to Konomi's lips. "You've certainly had a taste."

Heat rushed to my ears and I suddenly felt shy. "That's not what I meant."

"Are you blushing?" She patted my head again, her smile growing even wider. "You're so adorable and I'm greedy too. Remember what I said when we left the village?"

I swallowed hard. "You said you would stay with me, always."

Of course, I remembered. The words were seared into my brain, one of the many memories of hers that I wanted to see when my life flashed before my eyes.

She pressed her lips on mine again, smiling into

the kiss. "I meant it then and I mean it now. I'm yours."

Her words hit me in the spot in my chest where I always felt my wolf soul and I pulled her closer into me. I didn't have any words to explain just how much I loved her, but I didn't need to. I was sure she could feel this too, this new connection that was beautiful and tender and true.

THIRTEEN

The snow was fresh and shrieked under my shoes as I stepped out of the inn. It was so bright, I had to shield my eyes but it also meant we wouldn't be ambushed by a nasty storm before we reached the next village.

Konomi almost bumped into me and she grasped hold of my arm to stay upright. Even after a few days of being together, her touch still made my stomach flutter and I hoped that would never end.

A soft sob came from behind us and Rudy wiped the tears from his eyes with Mason's beard. "I'm going to miss you girls."

Mason wasn't nearly as emotional but he pressed a big pack of dried fruit into my hand and some of his favourite tobacco even though neither of us smoked. He claimed we'd be able to trade it but in my opinion, it seemed like he just wanted to give us a small piece of himself.

It was a strange farewell and reminded me a little of when we left the village, except that I barely knew these two men. I knew Konomi's charm was part of what had won them over so easily but I assumed the fact that I reminded Mason of his first crush had something to do with it too. If I had to hazard a guess, I suspected he'd been waiting for us. For the Guardian. After all these years, he still had so many unanswered questions and I hadn't been able to help him with those.

"We'll be back soon," Konomi promised.

I nodded. "When we return, we have to pass through here."

Rudy sobbed and pulled Konomi in a smothering hug. "You better return!"

The dullness in Mason's eyes told me he wasn't as optimistic. If his stories were true, if multiple Guardians had passed through here without any of them ever returning, he had a reason to be sceptical. Maybe the land beyond here was so dangerous, none of the Guardians survived. Or maybe they had even less reason than Konomi and I to return. I didn't know and I suspected that just like Mason, I would never find out.

It didn't matter. Whether it was danger or utopia awaiting us, I had an obligation to find out. To the village, to my family, and a little because I felt grateful. Without this sacred quest, Konomi and I might've lived our whole lives next to each other, always just missing out on this.

She turned to me, her hand held out. "Shall we?"

I nodded, easily slipping my hand in hers. I didn't know what was waiting for us over the next hill or even around the next bend of the path but we were going to find out *together*.

Rudy cried as we left and Konomi blinked a tear away too. She seemed sad to say goodbye and I had to admit to feeling a little weak in my stomach too. After all, the wonderful Red Boar Inn would always be the place where we found each other. It would always hold a fondness in my heart.

Konomi let out a happy sigh. "I love the snow. It's so beautiful and calm."

"It is," I agreed, briefly turning around to look at our tracks and the inn.

"What are you doing?" Konomi asked.

"Not sure," I admitted. "I think I'm fondly looking back."

She chuckled. "You're so weird sometimes. I love that about you. And I love that I can just tell you I love you now."

I pulled her towards me for a kiss. "I love you too."

The fresh snow compacted easily under my feet and slowly but surely, the inn faded from view.

Her smile was brighter than the sun. "You know, you never told me when you fell in love with me."

"I've been in love with you from the moment we met," I admitted as I thought back to the very moment when we met outside her house. I had a lot of memories of her and usually when I recalled them, they stung slightly but they no longer did. There was still yearning, sorrow, anger but I understood it all better now.

The fresh snow compacted easily under my feet and slowly but surely, the inn faded from view. Now it was just us again.

Konomi gave me a gentle nudge with her elbow. "What should we do when we find the Winter Stone?"

"What do you mean?"

"Should we have a party or something?"

I snorted. "I don't know. I think you're getting ahead of yourself. But sure, we can have a party."

A happy smile lifted Konomi's lips and she hummed a soft tune as she followed the winding path. It was just the two of us with the whole wide world ahead of us. The great unknown. I didn't know if we would ever find the Winter Stone or discover the mysteries surrounding it but for once, the future was beckoning.

Whatever came our way, we would face it together.

Thank you for reading Heart And Soul Of The Wolf. I hope you enjoyed Mayu and Konomi's story. While their romance is wrapped up, there's a lot more about their journey that didn't make it on page because this story is part of a bigger universe. This story is set many years before the start of the Guardian Of The Winter Stone and this is probably a little bit of a spoiler, but that story is about Akira, the new Guardian from their village to undertake the same quest.

If you want to know more about The Winter Stone,

their village, the Guardian selection process, and what became of Mayu and Konomi, you can discover all that and more in the Guardian Of The Winter Stone series. The first book is Duty Of The Winter Wolf and you can find it through this link: https://books.arizonatape.com/dutyofthewinterwolf

ABOUT THE AUTHOR

Ariana Jade/Arizona Tape lives her dream life hanging out with her dog and writing stories all day. Her favourite books to write are fantasy and paranormal romances with queer leads, stories that she wished were around when she was younger.

When she's not writing, she can be found cooking up a storm in the kitchen, watching shows that make her cry, or trying her hand at her new hobby of the week.

She currently lives in the United Kingdom with her girlfriend and her adorable dog who is the star of her newsletter.

Sign up here for adorable pictures, free books, and news about her books: www.arianajadeauthor.com/subscribe

Follow Ariana Jade

Website | Newsletter

- https://arianajadeauthor.com
- https://arianajadeauthor.com/subscribe

For more social media links, check out my website: https://www.arianajadeauthor.com/about

Follow Arizona Tape

Website | Newsletter

- https://www.arizonatape.com
- https://www.arizonatape.com/subscribe

For more social media links, check out my website: https://www.arizonatape.com/about-ari

OTHER BOOKS BY THE AUTHOR

Here are some recommendations on some of my other books you might like. My books are available on all retailers and can be requested in most public libraries.

You can find out more about each of my series on my website: https://www.arianajadeauthor.com or https://www.arizonatape.com

Cobblestone Coven

Down on her luck and with her magic no longer working, witch Cassiopeia returns to her small hometown to figure out what she truly wants from life. There's a lot to keep her occupied, from brewing hot drinks in her grandmother's coffee shop, to making potions to help out the locals, and a snarky talking cat. A cozy lighthearted fantasy.

Crescent Lake Shifters

Take a leap of faith with these dragon shifters looking for love. Only a jump in the Crescent Lake will reveal the bonds of fate. A paranormal romance series. Each book follows a different couple.

The Griffin Sanctuary

Help Charlotte take care of endangered mythical animals in the Griffin Sanctuary in this urban fantasy series. Perfect for animal and mythology lovers.

Queens Of Olympus

A modern paranormal romance take on the Greek gods and their dating life; it's not *all* drama. Each book follows a different couple.

Crescent Lake Bears

Jump in the lake of love with these bear shifters looking for their fated mates. Only the crescent moon will reveal what's meant to be. A paranormal romance series. Each book follows a different couple.

Guardian Of The Winter Stone

A fast-paced epic fantasy romance about a lone wolf shifter and her two fated mates on a quest for redemption, honour, and a sacred relic that holds the secrets about her past.

Cozy Fae Guides

As a chronically unlucky Fae, Naia's first adventure into the human realm will prove a real test. Saddled with the mission to amass as many riches as possible, she finds herself looking for something more valuable than simple treasures. A lighthearted cozy fantasy series.

Amethyst's Wand Shop Mysteries

An urban fantasy murder mystery series following a witch who teams up with a detective to solve murders. Each book includes a different murder.

Purple Oak Oasis

Find love and hope in this fantasy world with unusual magic. Each book follows a different couple. This series is co-written with Laura Greenwood.

For a full comprehensive list of all my books: www.arizonatape.com/all-series

Signed Paperback & Merchandise:

You can find signed paperbacks, hardcovers, and merchandise based on my series (including stickers, magnets, badges, and more!) via my website: www.arizonatape.com/shop

My website also has a selection of free stories and books that'll give you a taste of my other works: www.arizonatape.com/free

Printed in Dunstable, United Kingdom